This book belongs to

. . . .

First published in Great Britain 2005 as
No More Eee-orrh! by Egmont UK Limited.
This edition first published in 2015 by Egmont UK
The Yellow Building, 1 Nicholas Road, London W11 4AN.
www.egmont.co.uk

A CIP catalogue record for this title is
available from the British Library.

ISBN 978 1 4052 7814 0

Where's Your Eee-orrh?

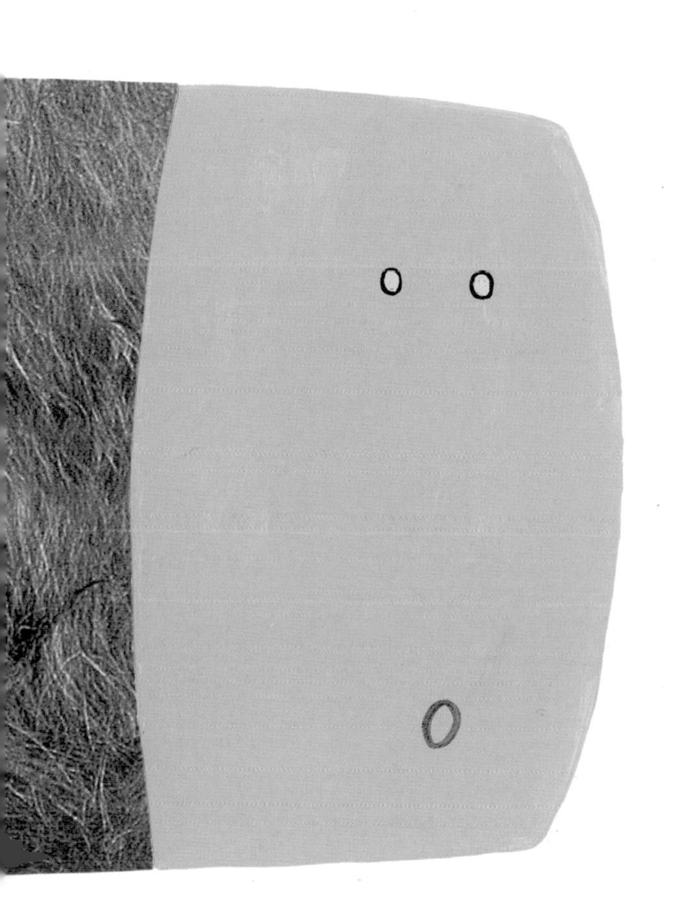

Lydia Monks

EGMONT

I don't need an alarm clock.
I've got **Dicky Donkey**.

Every morning, at the same time, he wakes me.

eEE-Orrh!
eEE-Orrh!

Our neighbours don't need an alarm clock either.
Every morning, at the same time, **Dicky Donkey** wakes them.

Miss Moany says the
noise niggles her nerves.

Mrs Moody says it makes
her brain boggle.

Mr Misery says it makes
his ears explode.

The other day they knocked
on my door to complain.
"**Dicky Donkey** has got to go!" they cried.
"NO!" I said. "NO!
NO!
NO!"

"Don't worry, **Dicky Donkey**," I said.
"I won't send you away,
no matter what they say."

Then yesterday I woke up late.
I knew something was wrong.

"Why didn't you wake me, **Dicky Donkey**?
Where's your eee-orrh gone?
Are you still worried about those
horrible people?"

But **Dicky Donkey** didn't answer.
He just looked sad.

I decided to take him to the animal hospital.
They'd know how to help him.

The doctor
took his temperature,

looked in his ears,

listened to his chest

and
peered
down
his
throat.

Then the doctor tried tickling him under the chin, while the nurse pulled funny faces.

But nothing would work.

So the nurse gave him
a donkey tonic
full of donkey goodness,
and tucked him up in bed.

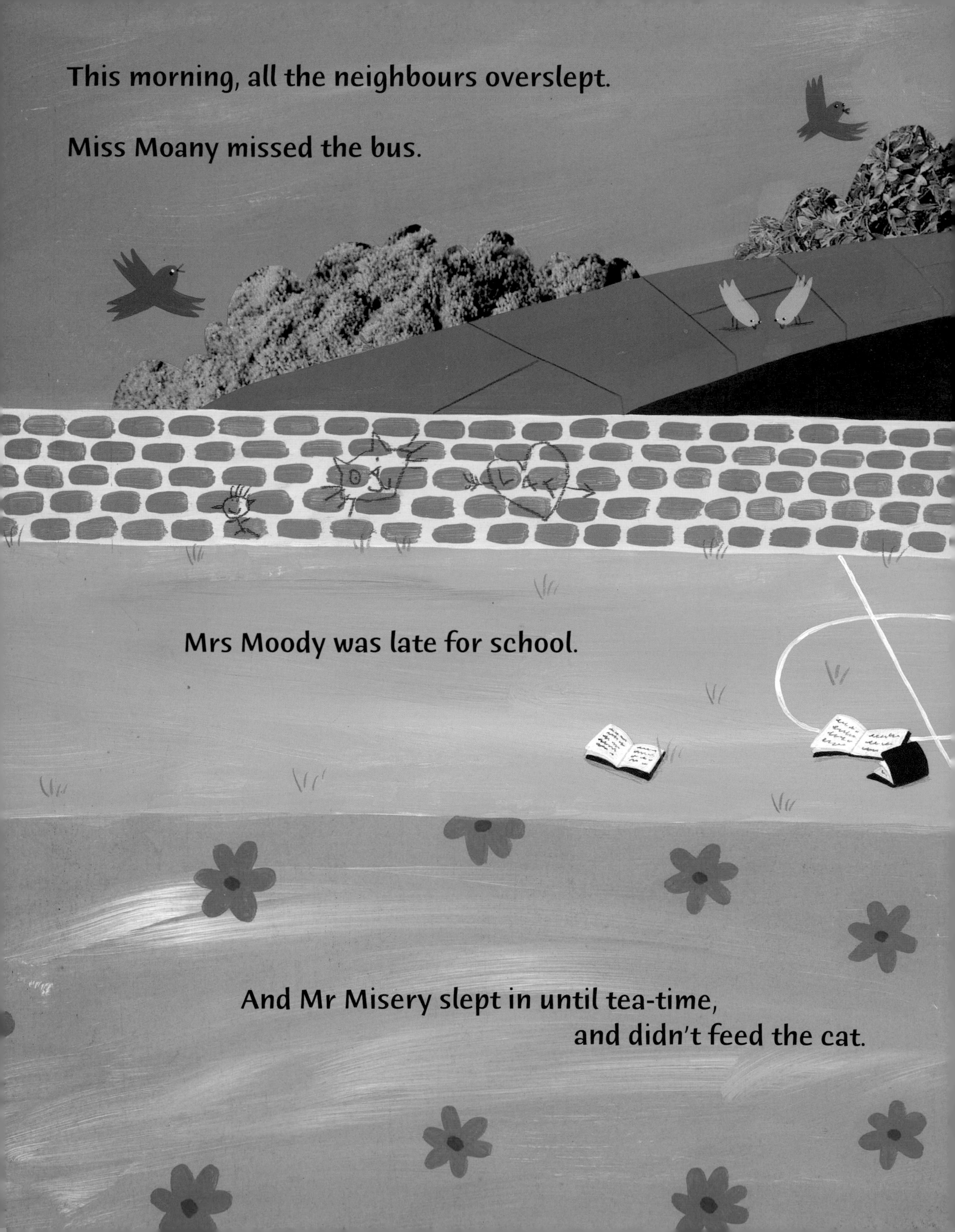

This morning, all the neighbours overslept.

Miss Moany missed the bus.

Mrs Moody was late for school.

And Mr Misery slept in until tea-time,
and didn't feed the cat.

"We need **Dicky Donkey** to wake us up!" said Miss Moany.
"It's our fault that he's gone," said Mrs Moody.
"How could we have been so mean to him?" said Mr Misery.

When the neighbours knocked on my door,
I told them where **Dicky Donkey** was.
We decided to visit him together.

Dicky Donkey was very surprised to see them.

"**Dicky Donkey**, please get better soon," they cried. "We miss our noisy neighbour!"

With that, **Dicky Donkey** leapt out of bed and . . .

eEE-Orrh!
eEE-Orrh!
eEE-Orrh!

EEE-Orrh!

"**Dicky Donkey** IS DEFINITELY BETTER," shouted the doctor, trying to be heard over the racket.

"He must go home STRAIGHT AWAY," bellowed the nurse.

Dicky Donkey was happy again.
He was so pleased to be going home.

And everyone at the hospital
was pleased he was going home too!